# Pursuing the Vampire!

## A Max Lovecraft/Lennie McMann Novel of the Paranormal

### Larry Scholl

©2023 All Rights Reserved

**No part of the contents of this book shall** be reproduced with the express permission of the author.

This is a work of fiction. Any resemblance between the characters portrayed in this novel and any persons living or dead is entirely coincidental. All situations are the product of the author's imagination and no resemblance between the events portrayed in this novel and any real-life experiences are intended.

ALSO, BY LARRY SCHOLL

AND AVAILABLE ON AMAZON.COM FOR KINDLE AND IN PAPERBACK:

UNDEAD: THE VAMPIRE OF KILLBRYDE CASTLE (ALSO IN HARDCOVER)

THE HOUSE WHERE I DIED

<u>FEATURING MAX LOVECRAFT AND</u>

<u>LENNIE MCMANN</u>

DEVIL'S NIGHT: THE HAUNTING OF FITZ MANSION

DON'T FEAR THE REAPER: THE HAUNTING OF ROOKWOOD ASYLUM

SUFFER, THE LITTLE CHILDREN: THE DEMON OF ST. XAVIER'S ORPHANAGE

DARK WATERS: THE HAUNTING OF LAKE LASALLE

THE KEEPER: THE HAUNTING OF BELLE POINTE LIGHTHOUSE

ZOMBIES AWAKEN (ALSO IN HARDCOVER)

NON-FICTION

TRUE STORIES OF HAUNTED PEOPLE, PLACES, AND THINGS VOLUME I

# Pursuing the Vampire!

## A Max Lovecraft/Lennie McMann Novel of the Paranormal

# Chapter One

It was a rainy night in Cleveland, Ohio. There were low rumbles of thunder and flashes of lightning on the horizon where the heart of the storm was raging.

Eleanor McMann, a world-renowned clairvoyant, called Lennie by her friends, had fallen asleep on the couch. The television was still playing, the bowl of popcorn she'd been snacking on had fallen off her lap and overturned on the rug.

The dream had begun innocently enough. A blustery night when scudding black clouds obscured the moon. An ornate Victorian house shaded by gnarled willows stood before her. She climbed the weathered steps to the porch but as she would have entered, a cold hand closed around her arm, the untrimmed nails digging into her flesh.

"Don't go in," a familiar voice said in her ear.

"Tobias?" She turned toward the voice and gasped, recoiling; only the icy grip on her arm keeping her from falling.

Tobias Craven, her old nemesis, a rival paranormal investigator and second-rate psychic who would stop at nothing to sabotage her success in the field, stood beside her, but she'd never seen him like that. He was usually expensively clad in a Saville Row suit that flattered his tall, elegant frame. But now his clothing was rumpled, stained. His face, though never full, was nearly skeletal, his lean cheeks were sunken, his eyes hollow.

"My God, Tobias, what happened to you?"

"Don't go in," he repeated.

"What is this place?" she asked. "Why shouldn't I go in?"

It was the ringing of her phone on the coffee table that brought her out of the dream. She checked the screen. It was Max Lovecraft, her fellow paranormal investigator and co-host of their popular television program 'Pursuing the Paranormal'.

She hesitated—trying to banish the last, clinging vestiges of the dream from her brain—before answering.

"Yes, Max," she said at last.

"There you are!" Max's chuckle sounded in her ear. "I thought I was going to have to leave a voicemail."

"I was sleeping."

"It's not even ten o'clock in Cleveland," he reminded her from his home in Los Angeles.

"What can I say, I'm a wild woman. I fell asleep watching tv."

"What were you watching? Not one of our old shows, I hope. That would just be sad."

"No, I never watch our old shows. I was watching the competition, the Van Helsing Brothers."

"You're not serious."

"They're funny."

*The Van Helsing Brothers* was a paranormal investigation team with a program on a rival network. There were three of them, Joey, Nate, and Ethan, who claimed to be direct descendants of Professor Abraham Van Helsing. When anyone pointed out that Abraham Van Helsing had been merely a product of Bram Stoker's imagination, a fictional character in *Dracula*, they insisted their ancestor had been very real and that Bram Stoker had merely based his character on him. The program was entertaining and the brothers had developed a loyal following so no one seemed to care if there was any shred of truth in their story. "Don't you think they're funny?" Lennie prompted.

"Not at the moment," Max told her. "They've gotten themselves mixed up in a mystery, perhaps even a murder, and they've asked for our help."

"We're not detectives, Max." Lennie noticed the spilled popcorn on the floor and, putting her phone on speaker, she laid it on the table and bent to sweep the kernels back into the bowl. "Tell them to call the police."

"Oh, they've been in touch with the police," he assured her. "Or rather the police have been in touch with them. They were investigating an urban legend in a small town in Michigan. Supposedly, the town is the home of a vampire. There have been disappearances over the years dating back to the mid-nineteenth century. And now there's been another. It would seem the Van Helsing brothers are the prime suspects."

"Why don't they just tell the police the vampire got him or her?"

"That's exactly what they told them. The police are, shall we say, skeptical."

"There's a surprise. Look, I'm sorry someone's missing, but we don't do vampires. Tell them to call Tobias Craven. He's always up for anything that might generate some publicity. You know, I was having a dream about him when you called—"

"They did call him," Max interrupted. "That's who's missing."

Lennie sat the bowl on the table and picked up her phone. "Tobias is the one who's missing?"

"They felt they were in over their heads. . ."

"In other words, they found something to convince them they were really dealing with the supernatural."

"Exactly. They contacted Tobias to come deal with the situation. He hasn't been seen since. You said you had a dream about him?"

"I was standing in front of an old Victorian house. The door was open. I was about to go inside when someone grabbed my arm. I turned around and it was Tobias. He warned me not to go in."

"That's all? Just don't go in?"

"You woke me up before he could say more. But he looked terrible, Max. Gaunt, pale, eyes sunken, cheeks hollow. . ."

"Like a vampire," Max finished.

Lennie felt a sick twisting in the pit of her stomach. "Yeah," she agreed dully, "like a vampire." She sighed. "I know what you're going to say, Max."

"We have to go, Lennie. A vampire? Come on!"

"After all Tobias Craven has done to us in the past, you still want to ride to the rescue?"

"It's not Tobias. You know I'd be the first one to serve him up to a vampire on a silver platter. But there's a mystery here. What did the Van Helsing brothers find that made them call Tobias in the first place? And where is he? Why did he look like a vampire in your dream? Do you get any sense of it? Any connections?"

"I don't know if clairvoyance works with vampires, Max. They're undead, you know. I usually work with actual dead people."

"Well then, here's your chance to meet someone new! You don't get out enough, Lennie. You need to meet new people."

Lennie rolled her eyes. Max's lectures on her love life, or lack of same, got old. "I don't want to sound picky, Max,

But breathing is sort of at the top of my list of attributes for romance."

Max laughed. "You told me once you were attracted to older men. According to the legends, this one's been around at least 175 years."

"Stop. You're killin' me here; you're so hilarious."

Max sobered. "All right. I'll stop. But say you'll come with me on this."

"Oh, all right, where and when?"

"Meet me in Detroit the day after tomorrow. I'll call and tell you what flight I'm taking from L.A. so you'll know what flight to book from Cleveland."

"All right. Goodnight, Max."

He chuckled. "This is gonna be great!"

Lennie put aside her phone. The memory of Tobias, disheveled, waxy, gaunt. . .yes, drained. . .in her dream came back to her. Somehow, she thought it was going to be anything but great. . .

## Chapter Two

Lennie spotted Max with ease amid the hustle and bustle of Detroit Metro Airport. He was the one in the midst of a crowd of adoring fans signing autographs and posing for pictures. From a safe distance, Lennie caught his eye and pointed to a coffee shop.

It was almost 20 minutes later that he joined her, towing his suitcase behind him.

"You should have come over," he said as he sat across from her and took a sip of the coffee he'd picked up at the counter on his way in. "Everyone was asking about you."

"I don't like being in the center of a crowd of strangers.

The impressions you pick up can be very weird, frightening even."

"I know." Over the years he'd become accustomed to the constraints her talents put on her.

"Where is everybody? Rafe? Alan? The equipment?"

Normally when they went on an investigation, they brought a cameraman, a sound technician, and a van load of equipment.

"It's just us. We're not filming this for the show."

"You're kidding! A vampire? We've never done anything like it."

"The Van Helsing brothers begged me to keep it between us."

"This is front page of the *Enquirer* stuff, Max, the publicity would benefit both our shows."

"They've lost Tobias Craven, Lennie. The man's missing."

She scoffed. "You say that like it's a bad thing."

"Seriously. I don't like him any more than you do but the fact remains that he's a world famous—"

"Asshole."

"That too. But he still has legions of fans whether he deserves them or not. If the Van Helsings are responsible for his disappearance, maybe even his death. . ." Max shrugged.

"Do we really want a piece of that? I'm still not sure it's a smart move on our part to get involved." She leaned closer.

"We'll be inserting ourselves into an active police investigation. If it comes to criminal charges, I don't want to be an accessory after the fact."

"First they have to find the body."

"Shhh!" Lennie smiled wanly at a passing police officer who cast a curious eye toward Max. "We're writing a novel, officer."

"Um-hmm," he grunted and went on his way.

"If he's a vampire, they'll have to find his coffin. Which means, we have to find it first."

"Oh damn! I forgot my stake and mallet. Do you have any garlic on you, Max?"

"Laugh it up." Max stood. "We'd better get going. I rented a car. It's about 75 miles north of here."

"You'd think the Van Helsings might have picked us up."

"The less attention we attract the better."

Lennie laughed. "Says the man who just posed for a couple dozen selfies and signed fifty autographs."

"More like a hundred autographs. But who's counting?"

Once in the car, Max followed the GPS instructions onto northbound I-75. Lennie waited until he had settled into the flow of light, mid-week traffic before asking:

"So, give me the gist of this story."

"All right. The town we're going to is called Salem Falls."

"Never heard of it."

"Not surprising. It's a wide spot in the road, at best. Farming community settled by German immigrants back in the early 1800's.

"One of the prominent families was the Rausch family, Lottie and Gustav, their sons Alex and Hans, and their daughter, Amalia. They prospered and built the biggest, showiest house in the area. It's a landmark of Victorian architecture even today.

"The son of a less prosperous neighbor began trying to court Amalia but her father disapproved. Apparently, this young man, Balthazar Emerick, was very handsome and charming but his family was comparatively poor by the standards of the Rausches.

"When the Civil War began, Balthazar decided to volunteer believing that if he came back a war hero, Amalia's father would look more favorably on him. Amalia, who was in love with him, promised to wait..."

"But he never came back?"

Max shook his head. "Oh, he came back. He joined the $6^{th}$ Michigan infantry. The last Amalia heard from him, he was in Baton Rouge, Louisiana. He disappeared after the Battle of Baton Rouge and was assumed killed. But then, after more than a year, he returned to Salem Falls and Amalia."

"But they didn't live happily ever after, I take it."

"Depends on what you call 'happily ever after' I guess."

"What do you mean?"

Max paused as he passed a slow-moving RV and steered the car back into the right lane.

"It seems the plantation owner who found him, wounded, after the battle, was a vampire. He took Balthazar back to his plantation but the young man was so near death that the only thing that could save him was to turn him into a vampire."

"And Balthazar agreed?"

"Who knows if he gave him a choice? In any event, he returned to Salem Falls a changed man. Seldom ventured out before sunset, was never seen to eat or drink regular food, avoided the rivers and falls that gave Salem Falls its name even though he'd been a strong and enthusiastic swimmer before he'd gone to war."

'Vampires avoid running water."

"Exactly. But he still wanted Amalia and she was still in love with him. But her father still disapproved, reasoning that any man who could not work outside was not going to make a success of farming."

"So, what did he do?"

"Coincidentally, a strange wasting disease seemed to break out in Amalia's family. First her brother Alex began to fail. He was weak, pale, eventually he wasted away and died. They buried him in the local cemetery."

"Coincidentally?" Lennie scoffed.

"Then Amalia's mother weakened and died. Then her other brother Hans."

"And her father?"

"He was found in the barn, hanged. They said he'd gone mad with grief at the loss of his sons and wife."

"Amalia had to have known Balthazar had something to do with it."

"No doubt. Reports from the time say she seemed to have a milder case of the disease that affected her family. She was deathly pale, wore dark glasses and long-sleeved, high-necked dresses to shield her skin and eyes from the sun."

"Balthazar was feeding on her. And she allowed it?"

Max shrugged. "She was in love with him."

"Standing by while someone kills your entire family and then letting him suck your blood seems a bit extreme."

"In any case, Amalia and Balthazar married and ran the farm with the help of hired labor. They seem to have had quite a turnover."

"Imagine that!"

"In the summer they hired migrant labor. At one time, a lot of the farms in the area hired Hispanic workers who would come up from Texas, mainly, and earn money working in the fields."

"I'm surprised word didn't spread about the death rate around here and make them go someplace else."

"Balthazar and Amalia Emerick paid very well. And at that time, it wasn't all that unusual for people to be walking around with what they called 'consumption'."

"Tuberculosis." Lennie nodded. "And the symptoms are not dissimilar to those of someone being fed on by a vampire."

"Correct. Fatigue, weight loss, no appetite, general weakness. It was rampant in the 19$^{th}$ century and the migrant workers generally kept to themselves so they probably suspected nothing." He put on the directional. "Here's our exit."

Nearly 45 minutes later, they were still driving on a two-lane highway with endless fields on either side. Corn, beans, sugar beets, potatoes, interrupted here and there by farmhouses, barns, and silos.

To one side, a lake appeared, blue and beautiful in the sunshine, stretching off into the distance, bordered by thick woods on each side. The two-lane road crossed a long bridge that was actually an old earthen embankment dam with gates that allowed water to spill into the wide river on the opposite side.

"Where is this place?" Lennie asked. "We've got to be halfway to Lake Huron by now."

"Not too far from it," Max agreed. "That's Salem Lake we just passed, it's man-made, the river was dammed back in the 19th century to allow a reliable flow of water for the sawmill in Salem Falls. The river flows through the town and empties into Lake Huron about 30 miles away."

"What about the falls? Salem Falls?"

"The falls are actually a spillway of the dam on the Salem River. At one time there was a sawmill on the river and a dam was built to divert water to turn the mill wheel. The mill burned back in the 20's but the dam is still there and the falls."

The GPS warned Max to turn and they crested a hill to see a town spread out in the valley below. A wide river flowed out of the woods to the west and curved through the town, sparkling as it tumbled over a dam that the main street ran across.

As they descended the hill, Lennie noticed a cemetery set back behind ornate wrought-iron gates. For such a small, isolated place, it seemed crowded with monuments. At the back, a mausoleum had been dug into a hill.

"Max, turn in there!" Lennie urged.

"We're supposed to meet the Van Helsings," he reminded her.

"Just for a minute," she insisted.

Max threaded the car between the open gates. The grave markers crowded close to the two-rut dirt lane that wound through the cemetery.

Many of the graves were topped by cement slabs or covered by iron cages.

"Mortsafes," Lennie said softly. She knew that they had been used in the 19$^{th}$ century to protect the dead from grave robbers. Most of the ones here, however, were surmounted by crucifixes and statues of angels.

"I never heard that there was a lot of grave robbing in this part of the country," Max murmured. "That tended to happen in cities where there were medical schools and they needed cadavers to dissect."

"I don't think these were built to keep people out," Lennie replied. "I think these were meant to keep the dead in their graves."

She reached out and touched his arm. "Stop the car, Max."

Max stopped in the shade of a gnarled oak tree that bore the scars of a long-ago lightning strike. Lennie opened the door and got out.

Walking between the old graves, she got the impression of great sadness, of grief and longing. Memories of lives interrupted flashed into her mind. Here and there a glimpse of a child lying surrounded by flowers and black-clad relations as a photographer prepared to record the scene. Memento mori, they were called, the ghoulish post-mortem photographs that were often the only image of the dead that were ever taken in an era when photography was new and expensive.

She saw a young woman, blushing and laughing in her wedding dress only to see another image of that same woman in that same dress, lying pale, cold, and still in a coffin while her husband of a few months wept.

She walked toward the back of the cemetery, toward the mausoleum buried in the hill. The entrance was covered with thick iron doors, the ornate handles were broken, the locks chiseled out. Vandals had long ago broken into the tomb and then the doors had been welded shut. Above the doors a stone had been engraved with the name, 'Rausch'.

Amalia's family. The first victims of Balthazar Emerick, taken with Amalia's knowledge and acquiescence in order that she and her lover might be together.

Lennie pressed her hands against the cold, weathered iron doors and closed her eyes. But she felt nothing. No uneasy souls lingered inside. The spirits of the unfortunate Rausch family had moved on to whatever awaited them beyond the veil that separated the living from the dead.

"Anything?" Max asked, coming to stand beside her.

Lennie shook her head. "Nothing. Which is strange. I would have expected Amalia at least to linger after the way she betrayed her family."

"That is odd," Max agreed.

"People were much more religious in those days. You would think that if she threw in her lot with an unholy creature and stood by while he murdered her entire family for their property, she might have some little flicker of guilt. But...wait a minute..."

"What is it?"

Without a word, Lennie started walking away from Max who, recognizing the signs, hurried after her. She stopped as suddenly as she'd begun, looked back in the direction she'd come from, and gasped.

"What did you see, Lennie?" he asked.

"Over there, under that tree." She pointed ahead of them. "I saw an apparition. It was Amalia, Max, I'm sure of it."

"There's no gravestone over there. In fact, I think that's outside the cemetery boundaries."

Lennie gazed toward the tree. While she'd been at the iron doors of the Rausch mausoleum, she'd felt a beckoning. Now, at the edge of the cemetery, in the shade of an old, dead, elm tree, she saw the figure of a woman dressed in an old wedding gown from the 19$^{th}$ century, dripping ancient lace, discolored and smeared with dried mud. The ghost held out skeletal hands, beseeching, begging, but not toward Lennie. Instead, she gestured toward a place behind Lennie.

When Lennie turned to look back, she had a fleeting glimpse of a man, in modern clothing, wearing a flat cap with the brim pulled low over a pair of oval dark glasses with shields attached to the bows at the sides of the lenses. But he seemed to have no interest in the pitiful, pleading phantom. Instead, he seemed to be watching her.

She looked toward the apparition then, when she looked back, the man had vanished.

"I'm certain it was Amalia," she said softly.

"Well, there's got to be a photograph or painting of her. When we find it, you can—"

"Won't help."

"Why not?"

"She had no head."

Max shuddered and laid a hand on her shoulder. "We'd better go now. We're late to meet the Van Helsings."

## Chapter Three

The park was a pretty, scenic place on the banks of the Salem River, north of town, not far from the dam. Surrounded by tall trees, it boasted a swing set, a few picnic tables and grills set in concrete, and a boat launch.

Two SUVs were parked near one of the tables. One was a large, new, dark blue one with a rental company sticker and the other an older one, painted dark gray with a light bar attached to the roof rack and a shield on the front door reading: "Portage County Sheriff".

The three Van Helsing brothers sat around the table along with a police officer in a dark gray uniform. They rose as Max pulled the car in beside the police car.

"There they are!" Ethan Van Helsing cried as Max and Lennie approached.

"What're their real last names?" Lennie whispered to Max.

"Who knows?" he answered. "They're the Van Helsing brothers."

Lennie had never seen three people who looked less like brothers than they did. Ethan, who was fast approaching, his hand outstretched, was a towering, blue-eyed blond who would not have been out of place in a Viking movie. Joey, shorter than Ethan by a good 8 inches, with his black curly hair, hazel eyes, and olive complexion looked like an extra out of an episode of the *Sopranos*, and Nate whose height fell somewhere between his 'brothers', was a muscular African-American man with a neatly-trimmed beard and moustache. The deputy rose and followed them at a distance.

"Wow! It is great to meet you!" Ethan said, enveloping Max in a crushing hug and then turning to Lennie. "Do you mind?"

She laughed. "Not at all."

Releasing Max, he wrapped his bear-like arms around her and lifted her off her feet.

"It was you guys who inspired us to start investigating," he told her when he'd put her back on the ground.

"That's great to hear," Lennie told him.

He pointed to the others. "This is Joey, and this is Nate."

Lennie and Max shook their hands in turn.

"You two are the best," Nate said quietly. "We've learned a lot from watching your show."

"Yeah, that investigation at the orphanage with the demon had me bricking myself," Joey added.

"Yeah, that one was pretty intense," Lennie agreed.

"They captured a demon!" Ethan said to the deputy who had come up beside them. "Imprisoned it in a Dybbuk box."

"A demon," the deputy said. "There really are demons?"

"Unfortunately," Lennie said. "But it wasn't just us. We had a former Vatican exorcist friend of ours with us."

"Did you say a *Vatican exorcist*?" The deputy's blue eyes were wide.

"Yes, the Vatican has a program for training exorcists. They don't advertise the fact, obviously, but they take demons and demonic occurrences very seriously."

"How do you know you're dealing with a demon?" he looked at Ethan and the other Van Helsings.

Joey scoffed. "Never met one myself, man. Don't want to."

"Where are my manners?" Ethan boomed. "Max, Lennie, this is Justin Leroux, deputy with the local sheriff's department. Justin, this is Max Lovecraft and Lennie McMann. He's a paranormal investigator like us...well, not like us, he's THE paranormal investigator! And this pretty lady is Lennie McMann. She's a clairvoyant."

The deputy shook hands with Max then turned to Lennie.

"Like a psychic?" he said, and his hesitation in holding out his hand toward her was obvious.

Lennie laughed. She'd encountered this reluctance more times than she could count. "Not like a mind-reader," she assured him. "Your whole life won't flash in front of my eyes if you shake my hand." She held out her hand and he shook it, smiling sheepishly. "I mostly deal with dead people anyway."

The look on his face made them all laugh and Ethan clapped him on the back.

"I love it!" he chuckled. "Shall we get down to business?"

They sat around the picnic table. Ethan placed his hand on a manila folder but as he would have opened it, Lennie stopped him.

"Before we go any further. I'd like to know about your role in all of this, Deputy. Generally, law enforcement doesn't approve or condone our investigations. But I don't think you would be here without authorization."

"I haven't got official authorization," he admitted, "but the sheriff knows I'm here."

"And he's ok with that?"

Justin shrugged. "It was his idea to call the Van Helsings in. Actually, his wife's idea. She's big into the supernatural; watches all the shows, yours, theirs," he nodded toward the Van Helsings, "pretty much all of them.

"The sheriff was under a lot of pressure to solve the disappearances and deaths that have happened in this area over the years. The sheriff before him wasn't able to, nor the sheriff before him, nor the one before him, you get the picture.

"His wife is convinced it's paranormal. She badgered him to call in investigators. He didn't want to because it's not exactly standard procedure and he didn't want to look like a kook. No offense."

"None taken," Lennie assured him.

"He assigned me to call in someone who would be discreet and promise not to publicize it. His wife wanted to call you in from the start but he thought it might attract too much attention. So, we called them, the Van Helsings. They called in Tobias Craven on their own. Then, when he disappeared, his wife insisted we call in what she called, 'the big guns'."

He looked at the Van Helsings. "No offense."

"None taken," Nate Van Helsing assured him.

"I'll be honest, Deputy. . ." Lennie began.

"Justin," he corrected.

"Justin, then. I'll be honest. Tobias Craven is a four-star asshole. . ." She paused while the Van Helsings laughed and nudged each other.

"We thought it was just us he didn't like," Joey exclaimed.

"No, he hates anyone with any success in the field. Trust me, if we manage to get him back, if he's even still alive, which I suspect he is because he came to me in a dream looking a little worse for the wear but very much still in this world, he'll try to take credit for the whole operation."

She turned back to Justin. "Anyway, I don't like Tobias Craven. I doubt that anyone who's ever met him likes Tobias Craven. And even if we manage to get to the bottom of this and get him back from wherever he is, he'll never agree to keep it quiet."

"But it will be all over by then, right?" Justin asked. "The disappearances and deaths will be solved and stop."

"I hope so. I've never dealt with a vampire before. As I said before, I mostly deal with dead people."

"He's not dead?"

"No, undead."

'But if it's Balthazar Emerick, he'd be over 150 years old."

"He looks pretty good for a man his age. I think I saw him today."

"What!" The combined shout of the men around the table startled the birds roosting in the surrounding trees.

"Lennie, you never said. . ." Max began.

"In the cemetery. I saw a man, he was dressed in modern clothing but he was covered, long sleeves, long pants, high collar, cap pulled down low, sunglasses with shields on the sides to keep the sunlight out of his eyes. I only saw him for a moment, then he was gone."

"I thought vampires couldn't come out in the light," Justin objected.

"To paraphrase Anne Rice's Lestat in *Interview with the Vampire*, 'the dark gift is different for each of us.' People tend to imbue vampires with the classic traits from Bram Stoker's *Dracula*, but the abilities and vulnerabilities seem to vary from case to case.

"Apparently, Balthazar Emerick can venture out in the daytime as long as he is well protected and the day is a little gloomy." She glanced toward the sky where the clouds seemed to be thicker now than they had been before.

"In the meantime," she said, leaning back. "I have a couple questions. "Why isn't Amalia in the family mausoleum and what happened to her head?"

## Chapter Four

The Van Helsing's whooped and high-fived one another while Justin Leroux sat still, a stunned look on his face.

"Awesome!" Ethan cried, nudging the deputy with his elbow. "See? I told you she's the real deal!"

"I see that," Justin murmured, looking at Lennie with a mixture of respect and, perhaps, a touch of fear.

"What happened," he went on, "was that in the '70s a group of teen-aged boys decided they were going to put this vampire business to bed once and for all. They didn't believe that Balthazar Emerick was still around; after all, they'd seen the man who lived at the old Rausch farm out in the daytime so he couldn't be a vampire, could he? Strange, perhaps, but surely not a vampire.

"And so, they reasoned, it must be Amalia. They went out to the cemetery and broke into the Rausch mausoleum. They broke open her coffin and found her mummified, I guess is what you could call it. They cut off her head and took it with them.

"The powers that be in town decided to move Amalia's corpse in secret to an unmarked grave outside the boundaries of the cemetery and weld the doors of the mausoleum shut so that people would think she was still inside.

"But one after another, the boys who had desecrated her corpse began to disappear. When there was only one left, he left the head on the steps of the police station and he and his family left town."

"Why was the head not returned to the grave?" Max asked.

"The other boys were, and are, still missing. It's evidence in an open investigation."

"Where is it now?" Nate Van Helsing wanted to know.

"At the police station in the evidence locker."

"I need to see it," Lennie told him.

"Why? It's just an old, withered-up severed head."

From the corner of her eye, Lennie saw the Van Helsings lean forward, anticipating her answer.

She didn't disappoint them. "I need to ask it some questions."

"Why didn't I see that coming?" the deputy sighed, while the Van Helsings and Max laughed. "All right, I'll talk to the sheriff."

****

The Van Helsings were staying in one of a half-dozen log tourist cabins ranged around a communal picnic area on the far side of the river from Salem Falls.

Max and Lennie had rented another of the cabins taking the skeleton key from the proprietor after a lengthy discussion about whether or not they'd brought any 'spooks' with them.

"As a rule, we leave them at home," Max told him.

The landlord, a short man with an enormous stomach that peeked out between the hem of his t-shirt and the waistband of his pants, laughed harder than the comment merited.

"Wait a dadgum minute!" he said as they were about to leave the office. "I'll bet you're here because of that other ghost guy, aren't you? The one who's missing."

"How did you know about him?" Lennie asked.

"Those old boys in cabin 3 were talking about him when I was in there tryin' to get the shower to work. He's dead by now. You might's well go on home."

"What makes you say that?"

"The vampire got him. Old You-Know-Who. . ."

"Voldemort?" Lennie asked.

"Funny. You know who I mean. I don't have to say his name."

"Balthazar Emerick."

"Shhh!" The man looked over his shoulder. "Don't attract his attention! I don't need no more of that trouble in my family!"

"You've had trouble with him in your family?"

"My great-granny. He bit her twice. She was never the same." He waved a hand. "Oh, I don't mean she turned into a bloodsucker, but she pined for him something awful. Now why would anybody do that, I wonder?"

"Strange," Max said, exchanging a glance with Lennie.

"It was. Mighty strange, if you ask me." He was clearly warming to his subject. "Yeah, she got so she'd go out at night hopin' he'd bite her again. Got so bad my great-grandaddy finally had her put in the state hospital up there in Traverse City."

"Amazing," Lennie replied.

"You betcha. But there's a lot of folks around here who had family bit by that sumbitch. They just don't talk about it."

"Why don't they do something about it?"

"Like what? Drive a stake through his heart? Got to find him first. He's out in the daytime; out in the nighttime. Besides, that's what you and those boys in cabin 3 are here for, aren't you?"

"Actually, we're here to find our colleague."

"Aw hell, he's likely dead by now. Maybe he's a bloodsucker too."

"Maybe so. Maybe we'll have to drive a stake through his heart too."

"You do that. Folks in this town would be grateful."

He looked around as a husky female voice shouted from the living quarters behind the office.

"Got to go, that's my dinner. You folks be careful now and don't bring any of them vampires home with you."

"We'll try not to," Max promised.

"We gonna git that sumbitch, Max?" Lennie asked, imitating the man's speech as they crossed the circular driveway toward their cabin.

"We gonna try," he insisted, chuckling.

But as they walked, a black SUV with darkly tinted windows passed the cabins on the two-lane highway at the end of the driveway. Against the background of a scarlet sunset, it slowed and the rear window slid partly open to reveal a pale face with piercing eyes that seemed to glitter in the dark depths of the vehicle's interior.

The window slid shut and the SUV disappeared down the road, but suddenly all the talk of vampires didn't seem a laughing matter anymore.

# Chapter Five

The next day, Lennie sat in a cinder-block-walled interrogation room at the sheriff's department located in the basement of the Salem Falls City Hall.

The door opened and Douglas Reichert, Portage County Sheriff, entered carrying a roughly one-foot square wooden box.

Sheriff Reichert was a tall, handsome man in his mid-fifties with salt-and-pepper hair and black-framed glasses.

He studied Lennie closely as he sat the box on the table before her, the hinged door of the box facing her.

"You sure you want to do this?" he asked. "It's not a pretty sight."

"I'm sure, sheriff," she replied. "But I've seen some pretty grisly things in my time."

"If you say so." His black brows drew together. "You're not what I was expecting."

"Really? What were you expecting. Wait, let me guess. A middle-aged woman with wild hair and flowy shawls, rings on every finger, and a black cat on her shoulder."

He chuckled. "Not quite. My wife made me. . .that is, I have watched your show on television before. I knew what you looked like. I just didn't expect you to seem so—"

"Normal?"

"Something like that." The levity left his face. "Listen, and I want you to impress this on your partner out there and those other guys, Moe, Larry, and Curly or whoever they are—"

Lennie giggled. She wondered how the Van Helsings would appreciate being compared to the Three Stooges.

"This," he went on, tapping the wooden box with his fingertip, "never happened. We at the Portage County Sheriff's Department, do not allow civilians to examine evidence in an ongoing investigation."

"Understood, sheriff," Lennie agreed. "But you know, don't you, what happened to the boys who broke into the Rausch mausoleum?"

"No, ma'am, officially, I do not. They've never been found."

"I see. Very well, sheriff, Max and I have agreed to make no reference to this investigation or anyone associated in any way with it. The Van Helsings have also agreed. No reference will be made to the matter either in any of our broadcasts or publications."

"I'll hold you to that, young lady."

"You can."

"Good." He turned to leave then hesitated, turning back. "Ah, my wife, you know, she's a big believer in all this stuff. She asked me to give you this."

He pulled a necklace from his pocket. At the end of a silver chain, hung an ornate crucifix Lennie recognized as a 'pardon crucifix'. From each of the cross-beams of the cross hung a medal. On one side, the miraculous medal of the Virgin Mary, on the other a medal of St. Benedict, said to, among other things, provide protection from the forces of darkness and demons.

"It's lovely," Lennie said, taking it from him and hanging it around her neck. "Please thank your wife for me."

"You can do it yourself," he answered, turning away once more. "Believe me, you're not getting out of this town without meeting her if she has anything to say about it."

"I'd like to meet her."

"All right, then. I'll leave you alone with Mrs. Emerick."

The door closed behind him and Lennie sat back in her chair, one hand absently closing around the silver crucifix around her neck.

She closed her eyes, drawing deep, calming breaths, clearing her mind of any thoughts of the world outside that small, windowless room.

"Amalia," she said softly. "Are you here with me?"

The room seemed suddenly charged with electricity. A hoarse voice rasped in her ear.

"Open the box."

Lennie undid the latch and swung open the front of the box. What she saw there made her gasp.

A human head, narrow, with a long, pointed chin, stared back at her from two deep black sockets, the eyeballs having decomposed long ago. The skin, stretched over the bones, had dried to the consistency and color of parchment, the veins, drained and dry, stood out beneath the flaking skin.

The thin-lipped mouth was partially open revealing stained teeth. The nose was aquiline, the nostrils flaring.

Lennie gazed at it. She hadn't known what to expect; perhaps something more. . .more dead. But this was no fleshless skull, a few strands of hair clinging to what was left of a scalp, still less was it a black, shriveled thing out of some Hollywood mummy movie. No, this was a recognizable face with gray hair covering the scalp, drawn back into a knot at the back of the shredded remains of the neck where it had been roughly severed from her body.

"Amalia," she said again. "I know you're here. I need to speak with you."

"I know why you are here," Amalia said in her ear, and Lennie half expected the narrow, cracked lips to move. "You want Balthazar. They all want Balthazar. They tempt him, flaunt themselves before him. But he is mine. He loves me. I am his wife."

"I don't want Balthazar," Lennie told her flatly.

What passed for laughter, dry, coarse, hissed in her ear.

"He wants you. You can talk to the dead. He is enthralled with the notion of how powerful you will be once you are transformed."

"Why did he not transform you?"

"Perhaps I did not want to be transformed!"

Lennie knew she had struck a nerve. After all those years of longing for him, finally marrying him at the cost of her family's lives, serving him, he had not thought to make her his eternal companion by making her a creature like himself. Rather, he had let old age claim her.

"I don't believe you, Amalia."

"Believe what you will!"

Lennie changed the subject not wanting to offend the spirit to the point where she refused to communicate further.

"How did Balthazar come to be transformed. Did he ever tell you that?"

"Yes," Amalia confirmed. "He had gone off to fight in the war of Southern Succession. He thought if he came home covered in glory, my father would relent and allow us to marry.

"He enlisted in the 6$^{th}$ Michigan Heavy Artillery in Kalamazoo. In 1863, they were sent to Louisiana. He fought at the Battle of Baton Rouge. Then they went to a place called Ponchatoula. He was gravely wounded in a skirmish.

"He regained consciousness surrounded by the dead and dying. It was night. All he knew was that he had to get off the battlefield before Confederate stragglers came back to finish off the wounded. Hateful creatures!

"He crawled off into the darkness, into the high weeds and trees. He heard someone coming toward him and thought he was about to be killed. But a man knelt beside him; a man in civilian garments. The man asked if he wanted to live, warned him that there would be a price to pay.

"Balthazar replied that he would pay any price to stay alive. And the man lifted him into his arms as if he were a feather and carried him through the darkness to his plantation."

"The man was a vampire and the price Balthazar had to pay was to become a vampire himself."

"Precisely."

"Do you know the name of this man or his plantation?"

"The plantation was Thornewood Hall and the man was Sebastian Thorne. He wanted Balthazar to be his companion. They went to New Orleans together, hunting."

"Why did Balthazar leave him?"

"Word of Abraham Lincoln's Emancipation Proclamation finally reached the slaves at Thornewood. Sebastian Thorne had known that slavery had ended but refused to free the people enslaved on his land. When they realized they had had the right to leave for more than a year, they rebelled. While he was sleeping, they broke into the room where he kept his coffin and decapitated him and burned the body."

"And Balthazar?"

"I do not think they realized he was a creature like Sebastian because he could appear in daylight. He took what gold he could find and a horse and escaped. The war had ended. Since he had been declared dead by the army, he couldn't be accused of desertion, so he came back to Michigan. Back to me."

"I don't mean any offense, Amalia," Lennie said tentatively, "but I'd like to ask you about—"

The door burst open and Max appeared. "Come on, Len, we've got to. . .holy shit!"

He stared, open mouthed, at the mummified head in the wooden box on the table in front of Lennie.

"Max! I'm trying to have a conversation here!"

"We've got to go. Now!"

"Why?"

"Sheriff Reichert just got a call from the state police. They're sending a detective over here to talk to him about Tobias' disappearance. He doesn't want a civilian in an interrogation room with evidence from an open case. We have to go."

Lennie rose and reluctantly closed the wooden box containing Amalia's head. As the left the room, she saw Sheriff Reichert looking anxious.

"Can I come back and talk to her some more another time?" she asked.

"Why not?" he sighed. "Just not now."

Max and Lennie left the building and climbed into Max's rental.

"You know, you could have been a little more subtle," she told him as they pulled out of the parking lot. "You probably offended her by yelling holy shit."

"Sorry, Lennie," he said, his tone irritated, "it's not often I come across someone—even you—having a heart to heart with a dried-up head in a box."

"It's what we do," she reminded him.

He nodded. "I could have been a lawyer, or a doctor, but noooo. . .."

Lennie laughed. "You know you love it."

"I do," he admitted. "So, tell me, what did your bodiless friend have to say?"

But Lennie didn't answer. Instead, she stared out the window at the blacked-out SUV parked in the parking lot across the street. As she stared, the back, passenger-side window slid down and she caught a glimpse of a pale face, the eyes covered by a pair of mirrored sunglasses with shields attached to the bows on the side.

"He's starting to piss me off with these games," she said softly.

Max said nothing. He knew from experience that pissing Lennie off was not a wise thing to do.

# Chapter Six

Grouped in front of the fireplace in Max and Lennie's cabin, the Van Helsings leaned forward, listening in fascinated silence as Lennie related the things Amalia had told her during their conversation at the sheriff's department.

"So, there are other vampires around?" Nate asked.

"Apparently so," Lennie confirmed. "Or at least there were back in the 19$^{th}$ century. There probably are others around today. I doubt Balthazar Emerick is unique."

"What was the name of that plantation she mentioned?" Ethan wanted to know, reaching for his laptop.

"Thornewood Hall, near Ponchatoula, Louisiana. Owner was a man named Sebastian Thorne."

"How do you spell Ponchatoula?"

"P-o-n-c-h-a-t-o-u-l-a."

"Okay, yes! Here it is. Thornewood Hall. It still exists. It says it was damaged by a fire in 1864. The owner, Sebastian Thorne, perished in the fire."

"According to Amalia, he didn't tell the people enslaved there that they'd been set free by the Emancipation Proclamation and had been illegally kept in bondage for a year and more. When they discovered they'd been duped, they attacked him during the day, while he slept."

"And what about Balthazar?"

"Amalia said Balthazar told her that because he could appear in the daytime, they didn't realize he was also a vampire. They just thought he was Sebastian's companion, a protector of sorts to govern the place while he slept. He seized his chance while they were rioting to escape and headed north."

Ethan was busy reading the article online about Thornewood Hall.

"This is interesting. The hall is open to the public like most of the old plantations down there. Oh! Listen to this!"

He leaned forward and read aloud:

"Like many Antebellum plantations in the area, Thornewood is not without its legends. Stories of spirits roaming the grounds and the breathtakingly-restored mansion abound but with a twist.

"In the case of Thornewood, the phantoms are said to be the ghosts of the victims of Sebastian Thorne, owner of the property during the Civil War years, who was rumored to have been a vampire."

"We have got to go there!" Joey exclaimed.

"By the time we're done here, you'll be sick of vampires," Lennie predicted.

"He's right, though, Len," Max said. "That place advertises that it was once the home of a vampire. We could do an investigation and actually do a show about it. Even write a book!"

"I don't know," Nate said, his face solemn. "Ghosts are one thing. This vampire stuff is really getting to me."

"It's not surprising, Lennie told him. "The last statistics I heard, almost half of all Americans believe in ghosts. They've become almost part of our day-to-day existence. But vampires are still the stuff of horror movies and superstition. Unlike ghosts, they have the power to kill us or to condemn us to an eternity of dwelling in the realm of nightmares."

"Yeah," Ethan said with a laugh. "Ghosts can't hurt us."

"Ah, but they can make us do things to hurt ourselves. A ghost startles you and you fall down a flight of stairs that's just as bad as if the ghost did it themselves," Max pointed out.

"That's true," Joey Van Helsing agreed. "But even so, we have Casper the Friendly Ghost, not Vlad the Congenial Vampire."

"Hey, don't forget Count Chocula!" Nate objected. "I love Count Chocula!"

"You got me there," Joey admitted. "I—"

"All right!" Lennie interrupted. "You guys! If this paranormal investigation thing doesn't work out, you could go into stand-up.

"What we're dealing with here, is a particularly dangerous vampire. Obviously, all vampires are dangerous, but most are vulnerable during daylight hours and need a protector, a Renfield, to watch over them during the day and keep anyone from harming them while they sleep.

"Balthazar Emerick, for some reason, can appear in the daylight house so long as he is dressed in concealing garments and wearing shaded sunglasses. That makes him unique as far as I know. It would be hard to attack him at any time of the day or night and be certain he would not be awake to defend himself."

"Then how do we do it?" Ethan Van Helsing asked, all levity suddenly gone.

A sudden, blue-white flash of lightning brought them all to their feet. After several seconds, a loud rumble of thunder seemed to shake the panes of the windows. The heavens opened and the rain, which had been threatening all day, poured down on Salem Falls.

"Anyway," Nate went on when they'd all sat back down. "Like Ethan said, how can we fight him when we can't attack him in daylight like a normal vampire."

"Normal vampire," Joey muttered. "Man, I just signed on to chase ghosts." He rose from his seat. "I'm going to bed."

"We have to plan what we're going to do about this guy," Nate reminded him.

Joey shook his head and the firelight glistened on his raven's-wing black curls. "When you figure it out, let me know. Cause I got no clue here."

The others were silent as he went to the door and disappeared into the rain, apparently not caring if he got soaked to the skin on the short walk to the Van Helsings' cabin next door.

"He's right, you know," Nate said, looked at Ethan. "We're over our heads here, man."

"Nah, we'll figure it out. Come on! One for all and all for one, right? Like the three musketeers."

"More like the three amigos," Nate groused. "Be honest, Ethan, we got into this because we used to watch shows like theirs. . ." He gestured toward Max and Lennie. "And we thought 90% of it was bullshit."

Ethan looked nervously toward Max and Lennie. "He's just tired, you guys."

"I'm not just tired," Nate told them and his dark eyes were deadly serious. "We figured we'd ham it up in our YouTube videos, build a following, then some network would give us a show. Hell, look at all the paranormal shows out there, most of them suck. But after we were stars on our own tv show, we'd be up to our necks in hot women." He nodded toward Max. "Be honest, man, you got hot women coming out of the woodwork, don't you?"

Max said nothing but Lennie laughed. "He knows Kandy Kayne. You know, Succubus of the Century from Dante Favarra's old nudie magazine *Dante's Inferno*."

"No way!" Ethan cried.

Nate laughed. "Is she. . .you know. . .good as she looks?"

"I just met her, you guys. We haven't even gone out. The magazine folded after Dante Favarra died and now she's performing in a show in Las Vegas. She came to a lecture I did in town and I met her at the meet and greet afterward. It turns out she's a fan of the show."

Max shot Lennie an exasperated look. Lennie smiled innocently back at him.

"Did she mention any other paranormal shows she likes?" Nate asked. "We do episodes in Las Vegas. Did she mention the *Van Helsing Brothers*?"

"No," Max said flatly. "Can we get back to how we're going to deal with this case, please?"

"Okay," Lennie said with a sigh as the pounding of the rain on the shingled roof nearly drowned out her voice. The lightning and thunder were almost simultaneous now.

"Because if not," Max continued, "I think it might be wise to pack it in for tonight. You guys are going to drown going back to your cabin."

The others nodded and Ethan and Nate disappeared into the deluge, their t-shirts pulled over their heads. Left behind, Max went into the bathroom while Lennie rummaged in the small kitchenette for a pan or kettle large enough to put under the leak that had appeared in the ceiling.

From the frequency of the drips, she knew it would be filled quickly and piled kitchen towels around it to try to soak up the overflow.

She sighed as she banked the fire in the fireplace. It was obvious that the Van Helsings were going to be of very little help. It was up to Max and her to defeat Balthazar Emerick and free the town of Salem Falls from his dominion.

But she was the first to acknowledge that she knew far more about hauntings and spirits than she knew about battling the undead. She'd learned some from their investigation of the La Croix plantation outside of New Orleans. But those had been zombies, not vampires. They were mindless, shambling creatures not powerful, cognizant beings who treated human beings as little more than their own personal playthings holding a godlike power of life and death over anyone they chose.

# Chapter Seven

Lennie lay awake listening to the rain on the roof. Even Max's snoring in the narrow twin bed beside her own could not compete with Nature's fury outside.

*Eleanor...*

She sat up in bed. "Tobias..." she whispered.

*Yes...*

Tobias Craven, the reason she had Max had been summoned to this place. The reason they found themselves involved with a creature that existed in that shadowy realm between life and death.

Lennie had never been particularly adept at psychic bonds with living people., Oh, she got images, impressions, sometimes when a person she met was particularly empathic, but most of her contact was with spirits, people who had crossed over, places where people had had overwhelming experiences that left strong psychic impressions on the very atmosphere of a place.

Tobias Craven was an exception. True, he was a clairvoyant, not as talented as she by a long shot but still, gifted with the ability to reach out with his mind and perceive things that were out of the dominion of ordinary people. Their minds could reach out to one another, connect, communicate.

*Are you here?* she asked with her mind.

*Not any more,* he replied.

*Was HE here?*

She heard Tobias' chuckle in her head. *He's never far.*

*Break away from him, Tobias. Help us fight against him.*

*It's not that simple.*

*Why not? He has to be destroyed; you know that.*

*I'm not that strong.*

*I don't understand.*

She heard him sigh, like the ripple of a breeze in her mind.

*No, you don't understand.*

*You can help us. Tell us when he is vulnerable. Tell me when it would be safe to approach him.*

*It's never safe. There are others.*

*Others? Like him? Other vampires?*

*No, he makes no other vampires. He wants no rivals. But he has minions who are in his power. They will protect him at any cost.*

*They must be eliminated before he can be defeated.*

*Yessss...* Tobias stretched out the word like the hissing of a snake.

*Where are they?*

*The house.*

*Why do they not escape him?*

*They are in his thrall. They love him slavishly. They would die to protect him and remain at his side.*

*Would you?*

Again, she heard him sigh and the sound was filled with longing and regret.

*I want to be free. And yet, I am fascinated by him. He is a creature such as I've never encountered. You know what our lives are like, Eleanor. We see angels and demons, lost souls and spirits caught between this world and the next. Fantastical things others without our gifts could never dream of. But I've never known anyone like him.*

*You sound like a man in love.*

*Perhaps I am, in a way. You cannot imagine what it's like.*

*What what's like?*

*To be taken by him; to feel his fangs penetrate your flesh, to feel your life force draining away and welcome it.*

*He feeds on you?*

*Of course, he has. It was frustrating for him.*

*Why?*

*He hoped to gain my powers of clairvoyance along with my blood. When he fed upon me, he got only a tiny glimpse of what it's like and only for a fleeting moment, and then it was gone. He thinks if he had a more powerful companion.*

. .

Lennie shuddered. *Me?*

*Yes, he knows my talent is a flicker, like the momentary glow of a firefly in the night; yours is a beacon. He believes that with you at his side, he would be all-powerful.*

*I would never be his companion!*

Tobias' laughter this time had a mocking air. *You say that now, but you can't imagine what it's like. . .*

*Enough! Will you help us or not?*

*Before you can hope to destroy him, you must eliminate his acolytes.*

*Will you help us do that?*

*Yes, I will help you. I must stop now. He's looking at me strangely.*

*You're with him now!*

*Of course. Where else would I be? Goodbye, Eleanor.*

*But wait. . .how. . ?*

But he was gone. Lennie could hear nothing but the pounding of the rain and the rolling of the thunder. Max lay unaware, unsuspecting, in the other bed.

Lennie lay back against her pillows, staring into the darkness, wincing when the blue-white flash of the lightning lit up the room.

Balthazar Emerick was feeding on Tobias and Tobias loved it. And he wanted to feed on her. He thought he could imbibe her gifts along with her blood.

She turned over and curled into a ball beneath the covers.

For the first time since she'd been very young, Lennie felt an emotion she didn't usually feel when it came to dealing with the paranormal—fear.


It was still raining when the cold, gray dawn broke although the storm itself had passed.

Lennie, who had fallen into a restless sleep not long before, groaned as a pounding on the cabin door shattered the calming patter of the rain on the roof.

Max threw back the covers on his bed and stumbled out of the bedroom. When he turned the knob, the door burst open and Ethan and Nate Van Helsing stumbled inside.

"He's gone!" Ethan cried. "When we went back to the cabin last night, it was dark and we thought Joey was asleep on the couch. But this morning we could see it was just bunched up blankets."

"What's going on?" Lennie asked, rubbing her eyes as she emerged from the bedroom.

"They say Joey is missing," Max told her.

"Well, maybe he just got up early and decided to walk down to the convenience store for something to eat or drink."

"No," Nate shook his head. "There's stuff on that couch that was there yesterday. He never slept there."

"So, he probably never made it back to the cabin after he left here," Max reasoned.

"What can have happened to him?" Ethan asked softly.

But as the four of them stood there in the shadowy living room of the cabin lit only by the weak light of the gray dawn outside, they knew what had happened to their friend and colleague.

Only Lennie was willing to put their fears into words.

"Balthazar took him."

"But why?" Nate asked, and his shock and fear were evident in his face.

"There are two possibilities I can see," Max told them, going to the tiny kitchenette to put some coffee on. "To frighten us into leaving here and leaving him alone. . ."

"Or?" Lennie prompted.

"Or," he continued, coming back into the living room and sitting beside her on the couch while the coffee brewed, "to lure us to him. Maybe he wants us to try and rescue him."

"We have to rescue him, that's a given!" Ethan declared. "I can't even imagine how terrified he must be! He was scared of this situation, you know. He was bugging us to just cut and run even before you guys got here." He shook his head. "When I think of him alone with that monster—"

"They're not alone," Lennie told him.

"How do you know?" Max asked from the kitchenette where he'd gone to prepare four cups of coffee. He brought them back to the living room and passed them out.

"I had a long talk with Tobias Craven last night."

"What!" Ethan and Nate nearly spilled their coffee. "He was here!"

"No, he wasn't here," Lennie replied. She raised a hand and touched her temple with her forefinger. "He was here."

"I thought you couldn't communicate that way with the living," Nate said. "Or is he. . ."

"Dead?" Lennie shook her head. "No, he's very much alive. He's a clairvoyant, you know."

"Not a very good one," Max muttered.

"Competent," Lennie admitted. "Anyway, we can communicate if we open our minds to one another."

"Did he tell you why he doesn't just walk away? There must be times when Balthazar is sleeping. Even if he can appear in the daytime; he's got to rest occasionally."

"I think he's in love with Balthazar."

"What!" Nate and Ethan were aghast.

"I didn't know Tobias was gay," Max observed.

Lennie laughed. "I don't know if he is or not. It doesn't matter, Max, this isn't about sex.

"Vampires are not like zombies, Max, they're not mindless killing machines. Throughout history, the vampire has been reputed to be an alluring, seductive creature. Once they get their hooks—or fangs, as it were—into someone, that person is under their spell. Mesmerized, captivated. Hell, Amalia Rausch Emerick is still enthralled by him after all these years and she's just a head in a frigging box.

"According to Tobias, Balthazar has acolytes—"

"He has what?" Ethan asked.

"Acolytes, followers, devotees, whatever you want to call it. People who are there for him, willing to protect him, feed him."

"Feed him?" Nate said faintly. "You mean they let him suck their blood? But I thought it a vampire bit you three times you became a vampire."

"Folklore," Lennie told him. "As long as a vampire doesn't drain a human of too much blood, they can go on feeding off them for as long as they want."

Ethan shuddered. "Do you think that's what he wants to do to Joey? Keep him as some sort of snack?"

"No, I don't think that," Lennie assured him. "Of course, that doesn't mean Balthazar hasn't fed off him. He probably has. If it has such a beguiling effect, he'd probably feed off him just to keep him submissive. He wouldn't try to escape."

"That bloodsucking bastard," Nate muttered. He turned on Ethan.

"We should have left like Joey wanted to! But no, it'll be good for the show, you said! Well, screw the show and screw you! I'm getting out of here!"

He rose but Ethan laid a hand on his arm. "Man, no, we can't leave Joey. You're right, we should have just left, but it's too late now. Sit down, man, we have to at least get Joey back and then. . ." He looked at Max and Lennie. "I'm sorry we got you here and sank you into this mess. But if we can get Joey back, we're out of here. If you want to trash us in the media, go ahead. This is above our pay grade, you guys."

"Maybe he's right, Lennie," Max said as Nate reluctantly sat back down. "If we can get Joey back, maybe you and I should just pack up and get out of Dodge too. This town's been dealing with this for over a hundred years. Let them figure it out themselves."

"I can't, Max," she said, shaking her head. "He wants me. That's why he took Tobias, to lure me here."

"Let him have Tobias," Max growled. "That guy's been a pain in the ass for years."

"Balthazar is convinced that the two of us could be very powerful together. Probably he's right. He won't rest until he has me by his side. And as long as he has Tobias, he can find me. I can try to close my mind to Tobias but I can't keep that up 24/7 indefinitely. Sooner or later, I'll relax and Tobias will make the connection and tell him where to find me. He won't risk turning Tobias into a vampire; no one knows if a clairvoyant's ability would survive such a transformation. But he'll keep him with him as long as possible. . ." She sighed. "Until one of us is dead and the connection is no longer viable."

"So, what does that mean?"

She looked into Max's eyes. "We have to end it, Max, here, now, in Salem Falls, or he'll pursue me, endlessly, relentlessly, waiting for his chance." She rubbed his arm.

"You don't have to be a part of this, you know. You can leave with them." She nodded toward the Van Helsings. "Go. Be safe. He doesn't want you."

"Don't talk stupid," Max said, slipping an arm around her shoulders and drawing her toward him. "Like I would leave you here to face this alone. I know I can be an asshole sometimes, Lennie, but I would never abandon you, and you know it."

"I know, Max," she admitted, as he kissed her temple. "I know it."

"Now, where do we go from here?"

# Chapter Eight

"There it is," Lennie said softly. "The epicenter of all the misery this town's endured for a hundred and fifty years."

Parked on the side of a country lane outside of Salem Falls, huddled under black umbrellas like mourners at a funeral on a gloomy day while the relentless rain poured down, Lennie, Max, and Nate and Ethan Van Helsing stared at the infamous Emerick House sitting majestically in the center of a large lawn.

Behind it there was a barn and several outbuildings but it was the house that captured the attention.

A classic Second Empire mansion, the ground floor was of red brick. The second floor and the two-story tall octagonal tower rising at one corner were hidden behind an elaborately patterned, slate-shingled mansard roof. Each window had a large hood, carved stone on the first floor, carved wood on the upper floors. Corbels abounded and the roof was finished with an ornate iron crest. The tower narrowed as it rose and the top was finished with what looked almost like an onion dome from some old Russian church. A columned pavilion framed the double doors with their leaded glass windows at the entrance.

A blacked-out Lincoln Navigator stood in the driveway.

"He's home," Lennie told them. "Balthazar. That's the car I see him driving around in."

"He's got Joey in there," Nate said softly. "We've got to get him out of there."

"Go knock on the door," Max told him, an impatient edge to his voice. "Tell him you want your friend back."

"That'll work out well," Nate muttered.

"It might," a voice said from behind them.

The turned to find the deputy, Justin Leroux walking up to them. Absorbed in their perusal of the house, they hadn't heard his police SUV approaching.

"I've done it," he said, coming to stand beside Lennie. She raised her umbrella so he could join her underneath it. "We got a call that a group of suspicious strangers were standing out here casing the house."

"Casing the house?" Ethan said. "Balthazar called the police on us?"

"Suspicious strangers?" Lennie asked. "Come on, he knows exactly who we are, and why we're here. And what do you mean, you've done it?"

"He's got Joey in there," Nate told him. "He took him last night."

"I've gone up and knocked on the door. He's got my sister, too," Justin told him.

"He what!" Max exclaimed.

Justin nodded. "My younger sister, Melanie. Years ago, when she was 15, she and some friends went out on gate night—you know, the night before Halloween. They were going to pull some pranks, toilet paper some trees, smash some pumpkins, typical kid stuff.

"Apparently, someone bet her a hundred bucks she wouldn't go up on that porch and knock on the door."

"And she did it?" Ethan asked.

Justin smiled wanly. "My sister was—is—no shrinking violet. The kids said she went up onto the porch and knocked. The door opened and someone they couldn't see beckoned her inside. She called back to ask what they'd give her if she went inside. One of them said two hundred bucks and she stepped inside." He sighed. "She didn't come back out."

"And that's when you knocked on the door?" Lennie asked.

He nodded. "I hadn't been a deputy very long. I went up to the door and some guy answered. About my age, in his 20's. I told him I was there for my sister. I reminded him she was underage and I could get the FBI involved for kidnapping, trafficking, whatever.

"He disappeared for a while and then the door opened and my sister was shoved out onto the porch. She pounded on the door, screaming to be let back in. I had to cuff her and carry her to my squad car."

"Had he—" Lennie began.

"Fed on her? Yes, I believe so. There were healing scars on her wrist. She denied it, of course. She was put under observation in a mental health facility. She stayed there for almost three years because she refused to acknowledge anything untoward that had happened at the house. Denied even knowing Balthazar Emerick. But when she was finally released, she came home for a few months. On the night she turned 18, she disappeared."

"She was of age and went back to Balthazar," Lennie said.

"We believe so. But, she's legally an adult now and we have no probable cause to believe she's being held there against her will, so there's nothing we can do."

He sighed. "Which brings me to my business here. Do you have any proof that your friend is inside that house?"

"Proof," Nate asked. "No, no solid proof."

"Did any of you see Balthazar Emerick take him?"

"No," Ethan admitted. "He was just gone. But I know it was—"

"Knowing isn't proof," Justin reminded him. "And until you have proof that he's been kidnapped and is being held under duress, it is my duty to ask you to move along."

It was two in the morning with the rain still pouring down on the moss-spotted wooden shingles of the cabin roof when the pounding on the door woke Lennie and Max from a sound sleep.

Max stumbled to the door while Lennie searched under her bed for her slippers. When she emerged into the sitting room where the last embers of a fire built to dispel the pervading damp glimmered in the hearth, Max was trying to calm a near-hysterical Ethan Van Helsing.

"You've got to come!" he said, grasping Max's arms and shaking him. "Please! You've got to help him!"

"Ethan! Help who?" Lennie demanded.

"Joey! They brought him back! That black Escalade pulled up outside and the door opened and they pushed him out! We were still awake and we heard him screaming!"

"Screaming! What were they doing to him?" Max demanded.

"Nothing! That's just it! They were trying to leave but he had ahold of the wrist of the guy who pushed him out of the back seat. He was trying to get back in!"

"Are you serious?" Lennie asked.

"As a heart attack! The guy finally put a boot in Joey's chest and kicked him into the mud! The car door slammed and they drove off."

"Did you get a look at the guy?" Max asked.

Ethan shook his head. "Just a pale face with scary eyes. Please! Come and see if there's anything you can do to calm him down."

Max and Lennie pulled on shoes to protect them from the mud and, huddled under a single umbrella, ventured out into the chilling rain. Even so, they were all soaked when they reached the neighboring cabin. The rain was blowing almost horizontally across the muddy drive.

Inside the cabin, Nate stood over Joey who was recumbent on the sofa. When Max and Lennie approached, they saw that his arm was tied with the belt of someone's robe to the leg of the heavy sofa.

"You tied him up?" Lennie asked.

"Had to," Nate replied. "He's crazy!"

Joey regarded them with wild eyes in a pallid face. Tears were streaming down his cheeks.

"Let me go. . ." he whimpered. "Please, please, I have to go back. . ."

"Joey," Lennie said softly, kneeling beside him. "They let you go. You're free."

"I don't want to be free!" he screamed. "I want to go back!"

"Joey," Lennie began, taking his free hand. "Why in the world would you want—"

She gasped as she saw the half-circle of blood-clotted toothmarks on the outside of his hand. "He fed on you," she breathed. "Was it Balthazar?"

"Balthazar," Joey whispered, his eyes wild in his face. "Yes, Balthazar." His hazel eyes were filled with tears as his fingers clutched at her arm. "He will think I ran away from him. Help me, Lennie, help me go back to him."

"Joey," she whispered, "Joey, he has you in his power but if you go back, he will destroy you."

"No," Joey shook his head. "He loves me, I know it. You don't understand; you can never understand. . ."

Lennie rose. "I don't know what to tell you," she said, looking up at the anxious faces of the other two Van Helsing brothers. "Remember what Justin told us about his sister.

She was in a mental health facility for three years after they got her away from Balthazar. The minute she turned 18 and could do as she liked; she went back to him."

"So, he's doomed?" Nate asked. "For the rest of his life he's going to be like this? Desperate to get back to that monster?"

"Don't call him that!" Joey cried, struggling.

Lennie gestured for the others to follow her outside. "Keep an eye on him, will you, Max?" she said.

She led Nate and Ethan outside and closed the door so Joey could not hear her. They crowded together under the small awning over the door to shield them from the relentless rain. "I don't know about this," she admitted. "This is as much new territory for me as it is for you. It looks like Balthazar only fed on him once, so perhaps with time Joey will recover. After all, Justin's sister was with him for a long time before they got her out, so there was probably little chance that the virus or curse or whatever he infects his victims with when he feeds on them, would dissipate over time. With Joey, if he was only infected once, perhaps with time he'll get over it."

"You make it sound like the flu," Nate snapped.

"I don't know what it is!" Lennie growled. "I'm a clairvoyant, that doesn't mean I know everything there is to know about every supernatural creature that's ever walked this earth.

"You have no idea what it's like!" She jabbed a finger into his chest. "I've spent my life seeing monsters. I spent two years of my like in an asylum—they call it a 'mental health facility' because everyone is so damned politically correct—but it was a lunatic asylum, a repository for people who had gone over the edge, a place where they throw drugs at you and claim you're cured. They said I'd gotten over my 'delusions' about seeing spirits and talking to spirits, but I never did. Not a day went by while I was in there that I didn't see some lost soul pleading for my help, or some demon threatening my soul. I denied it just so I could get out, but it never stopped.

"I'm doing the best I can here, but this creature is so evil, and so powerful, he could well destroy us all before he's done. You came here thinking you could garner ratings for your show by exploiting the people he's been victimizing for over a century. You didn't think he was real, did you? Because you're not real. You're not paranormal investigators, you just jumped on the bandwagon when they were handing out television shows to everyone with a gimmick.

"But now you see that there is real evil in the world. There are real supernatural creatures. So, you call me in because you know I'm as real as they are. You dump this in my lap and expect me to vanquish it like some paranormal superhero. Well, I don't know how, all right? I—don't—

know—how! I'm trying to figure it out as I go along so maybe you could cut me a little fucking slack!"

Nate and Ethan looked sheepish and said nothing. Lennie opened the cabin door to find Max sitting on the sofa beside a shivering, whimpering Joey.

"Come on, Max," she said. "There's nothing I can do tonight. These guys will just have to watch him and we'll try to figure something out in the morning."

The next morning, Lennie was sitting at the table staring out at the rain, idly stirring a cup of coffee when Max who'd gone to check on Joey and the others, appeared in the doorway.

"They're gone," he said flatly, casting a grim look up at the ceiling as a rumble of thunder broke overhead.

"The Van Helsings?" Lennie nodded, taking a long sip of her coffee. "I'm not surprised. They've had a nasty shock.

They've just discovered that the paranormal isn't like *Ghostbusters*. They thought they'd get rich and famous off something that wasn't real and then it turned out to be real after all."

"We could do the same, you know," Max told her. "Just pack up and leave. This isn't our problem, Lennie. This creature has been here for over a century. For all we know he could be immortal. There'll be plenty of opportunities for someone to destroy him in the future. It doesn't have to be us."

"And what about Tobias?"

"What about him? He's been no friend of ours. How do you know this isn't all just some bargain he's made with the devil to get you out of the way?"

Lennie shook her head. "I don't think it is. I think he came here to help the Van Helsings believing it would spawn another bestseller for him, make him front-page news again, and discovered that Balthazar Emerick wanted to use him as bait to get to me."

"So, he'll end up just like Joey? Just like Justin's sister?"

"No, he told me Balthazar had fed on him once and was disappointed that he didn't absorb Tobias's powers of clairvoyance along with his blood. But it must have been a powerful experience. You can hear the longing in Tobias's voice when he talks of it. He would willingly allow Balthazar to feed on him again."

"You sound as if you're curious about it," Max said warily.

"I am curious. This is all uncharted territory, Max. All my life I've know the paranormal was real. I've known there were ghosts and demons and creatures most people believe are only in stories or movies. But vampires. . .even I didn't know there were really vampires.

"For all his evil, Balthazar Emerick is a fascinating creature. I wish I could talk to him."

"Without teeth in the neck being involved, of course."

Lennie laughed. "Of course."

Lightning struck a tree not far away with a deafening crash and Lennie and Max both jumped.

"Isn't this rain ever going to stop?" he growled.

"Doesn't seem like it."

"Where do we go from here?"

Lennie sighed and poured herself another cup of coffee.

"Where, indeed?" she asked.

# Chapter Nine

"Our Lady of Sorrows," Lennie read. The words were carved on the base of a tall statue of the Virgin Mary, her hands turned out in supplication and her eyes downcast.

Lennie and Max had driven to the next town, Edenton, which lay about 15 miles from Salem Falls. Max had gone to the historical society to see if he could discover if there had been any unexplained disappearances there in the last 150 years and Lennie had decided to visit the local Catholic church and see what the priest had to say about the rumors that must have reached his ears about an evil presence in the neighboring town.

Lennie closed her umbrella and shook the rain droplets from it as she reached for the massive door handle. The iron door hinges groaned as she opened the oversized door and stepped into the fragrant darkness of the vestibule.

Our Lady of Sorrows, so the cornerstone of the soaring church read, had been begun in 1882. A display in the vestibule showed a grainy black and white picture of a white clapboard church that had apparently been replaced by the little stone cathedral as the area became more prosperous thanks to logging fortunes.

Lennie leaned her umbrella against the wall as she moved toward the sanctuary, she unconsciously dipped her fingers into the holy water font and made the sign of the cross. Her parents hadn't attended church with any regularity when she was a child, but her father worked occasionally with priests and Catholic exorcists and thought highly of the fact that the Catholic church considered demons and possession as factual more than most Protestant religions.

This particular church, she was pleased to see, had apparently resisted the modernization that had seen so many ornate churches modified and simplified over the years. The intricately carved altarpiece soared into the shadows of the vaulted stone ceiling and the rows of polished pews with their knee-punishing kneelers stood in silent rows awaiting the faithful.

Candles burned on the altar and in front of the tabernacle and the smell of incense hung in the air. At the side of the church was a row of wooden confessionals. The curtain was drawn on one side of one pair but not the other and no one sat in the pews waiting their turn so Lennie assumed the priest inside was not occupied.

"Father Bauer?" she said, having seen his name on the sign outside the church. She knocked lightly on the wood of the confessional. "Father, I'm not here for confession but I would like to speak with you if you have a few moments."

There was no reply. She tried again.

"Father Bauer? Are you there? My name is Eleanor McMann and I would like to speak to you if you have a bit of time to spare."

Again, there was no reply, but Lennie heard a slight movement from inside and a foot shod in black leather slid out from beneath the curtain.

"Father," Lennie said, alarmed, "are you all—"

She pulled back the curtain. A small scream escaped her as she jumped back in horror.

Father Aloysius Bauer, 62, who had devoted nearly his entire life to the church he loved, to the God he worshipped, to the good he devoutly believed would triumph over all the evil in the world, sat in his chair, his head slumped against the carved screen that separated him from the penitents he counseled in the adjoining booth on so many occasions.

His black vestments were draped around him. His arm hung loosely at his side, the other rested on the shelf below the grille having knocked his bible to the floor. A black beaded rosary dangled from his fingers.

His white collar was stained red with blood from the two ragged holes in his throat. Blood had soaked into the purple silk of his stole staining it with what looked like black smears.

"Father Bauer!" Lennie breathed, reaching toward him.

"I'll call—"

"No one," a voice said softly from behind her.

Lennie whirled toward the voice, a scream dying I her throat as she found herself trapped between the dead priest and the tall vampire.

Dressed in black, Balthazar Emerick towered over Lennie.

He must have been well over six feet, unusually tall for a man born in the early decades of the 19th century. His hair was dark with a white streak like a bolt of lightning at each temple. His skin was pale, stretched taut over the sculpted planes of his face. His eyes, without the concealing sunglasses he normally wore, were almost violet although when he turned his face toward the candles, they seemed redder and when he turned away from the light, they seemed to take on a blue cast.

"Balthazar Emerick," Lennie whispered.

He smiled and she saw the gleam of his teeth, the canines long and pointed.

"Yes, Eleanor, at last we meet."

Lennie glanced back at the twisted corpse in the confessional. "Why did you have to kill him?"

Balthazar shrugged. "I didn't."

"Are you denying—"

"I didn't HAVE to," he corrected. "He was very old, you know, and his health was failing. He has a cancerous tumor beginning in his brain although he didn't know it yet. Inoperable. I saved him a great deal of pain and suffering."

"You're a regular Mother Theresa," Lennie snapped.

Balthazar laughed and the sound sent shivers down Lennie's spine.

"I have my moments."

"How did you know I was here?"

"Tobias told me. He said you'd been blocking your thoughts from him but last night he managed to see into your mind and he saw that you intended to come here today."

"I thought it was time we met."

"Are you going to kill me as you did Father Bauer?"

Balthazar made a dismissive gesture. "Forget about Father Bauer. He's probably in Heaven by now strumming a harp.

But no, of course I'm not going to kill you. You are a rare and precious creature. I want to learn from you. I want to see the world, this one and the next, as you see it."

"And if I don't want to show you my world?"

"I can be very persuasive."

He moved very close to her and Lennie smelled the musky, seductive scent of him. She had imagined that an undead creature like this would smell of the tomb, of damp and decay, but his scent was like a rainy night in a forest, of exotic, night-blooming flowers and mountain juniper.

Lennie felt her pulse quicken and heard his soft sound of pleasure at the sight of her arteries throbbing in her neck.

He took her hand and she felt the coldness of his skin reminding her that the creature who stood before her was neither alive nor dead but in some unholy limbo between the two. He had no heartbeat of his own, no blood of his own pumping through his veins, and yet his flesh did not decay and turn to dust though more than a century had passed since he was truly alive.

He raised her hand to his lips and Lennie held her breath, remembering the bloody marks on Joey's hand where he had been bitten. But as he turned her hand over, her fingertips grazed his flesh and he hissed, dropping her hand and stumbling back. He cast an angry glance down at his own hand and Lennie saw strange, scaly marks, like fingerprints appear on his flesh. She realized it was where her fingertips, dipped so recently in the holy water at the door of the Sanctuary, had touched him.

"How can you be inside of a church with impunity and yet be burned by the remnants of the holy water on my skin?" she asked him. "How could you put your hands on a priest, tear out his throat with your teeth, without harming yourself?"

"The priest had sins of his own," Balthazar replied, "unresolved sins, unconfessed, unforgiven. . . He was not in a state of Grace. The water is pure, blessed, and you. . .you with your gifts of touching the other world. . .are beloved by the denizens of Heaven."

"And yet you seek to defile me."

Balthazar shrugged. "Perhaps I seek to gain some of that Grace for myself."

"Is that possible? You are a creature of death. You have killed countless people. Is it possible for you to attain a state of Grace?"

"I am a sinner," he admitted. "I covet. . .I covet your power; I covet your innocence. Could your blood imbue me with some share in that power? Some return to innocence? Shall we find out?"

His hand darted out and, wrapping around the back of her neck, pulled her against him.

Lennie was shocked for a moment, paralyzed, but when she felt his cold breath on her throat, she raised her hand and pressed her fingertips against his cheek.

He hissed and stepped back. The same marks that had appeared on his hand now marred the pale smoothness of his cheek.

"Lennie?" Max's voice shattered the silence in the sanctuary. He appeared in the doorway and stared, stunned to see her standing there so close to Balthazar Emerick.

"We'll meet again," Balthazar told her, and was gone, moving too quickly for them to follow, leaving them alone in the church with the ravaged corpse of the old priest.

# Chapter Ten

Lennie leaned her head back against the headrest as they drove through the rain back to Salem Falls.

"Do you think they believed me?" she asked, staring out the window at the sodden scenery they were passing.

"Do you think they would have believed you if you'd told them the truth?" Max countered.

Having been seen entering the church and knowing they would likely be seen leaving, Max and Lennie had decided they had no choice but to notify the authorities of Father Bauer's murder.

The police had swarmed the church and a stern-faced detective had taken them to the local police station where they'd been questioned.

Lennie had told them she'd entered the church to make confession to Father Bauer and had found him dead in the confessional. Max had told them he'd gone to the historical society to research local history and, when he'd finished, he'd gone to find Lennie. She'd been in shock, dumbfounded by the horrible sight of the bloodied priest, and he had phoned the police while trying to comfort her.

The detective, a man of long experience and seasoned instincts, had obviously believed there was more to the story than what they were telling him, but there was no evidence that either of them had touched the old man.

He'd told them they could go but cautioned them not to go far pending the results of the postmortem. They had given him their telephone numbers and told him where they were staying, and assured him they would be in the area for the foreseeable future.

"I could hardly tell him I had stumbled onto a vampire attack, could I?"

"Maybe," Max reasoned. "The lady at the historical society was reluctant to talk about it, but there have been disappearances in and around Edenton over the years just like in Salem Falls. Young people, having heard the stories of Balthazar Emerick, dare one another to go to his house and are never seen again.

"The police class them as runaways."

Lennie scoffed. "Of course, they do. That's how he's survived all these years. But he's not invulnerable, Max. The holy water on my fingertips burned his hand and his face. He can be destroyed."

"Let Tobias destroy him!" Max snapped, frowning. "Let someone fifty years from now destroy him! A hundred years! Two hundred!"

"Max..."

"Christ, Lennie, I thought my heart would stop when I spotted you with him! What if you can't destroy him? What if he destroys you?"

"He could have destroyed me today, Max," Lennie reminded him. "He doesn't want to."

"Because he wants you for his mate or companion or something. What's our next book going to be? *Bride of the Vampire?*"

"He thinks he can absorb my psychic ability along with my blood. Apparently when he feeds on Tobias, he temporarily gains a small amount of clairvoyance."

Max scoffed. "Because that's all Tobias has. . .a small amount. Imagine, Lennie, if he was psychic on top of his other powers."

"I know, he'd be so—"

Oh, no," Max groaned as they turned into the parking lot of the motel. "Out of the frying pan and into the fire."

A sheriff's department SUV stood in front of their cabin; the windshield wipers turned off. But as they approached, the wipers turned on and the door opened.

Justin Leroux, wearing a black rain jacket with POLICE spelled out across the back and a hat covered in protective plastic, got out and came toward them as they exited the car.

"Come in out of this damned rain," Max invited, as Lenne ran ahead to unlock the door.

The door of the next cabin was open and a housekeeping cart could be seen just inside the door.

"The Van Helsings?" Justin asked, as the three of them shed their rain spattered outer clothes and hung them to dry on the coat rack beside the door.

"Gone," Lennie told him. "Coffee?"

"Sure, thanks," Justin replied.

"Please," Max added.

When the three of them were ensconced on the sofa, a mug of steaming coffee in their hands, Justin was the first to speak.

"Sheriff Reichert asked me to come and talk to you. He's heard about the old priest over in Edenton. They're calling it a heart attack."

"Heart attack!" Lennie cried. "His throat was torn out!"

"No doubt, but still, that's going to be the official verdict from the county coroner."

"That's the local euphemism, is it?" Max shook his head, exasperated. "Justin, this monster has been controlling this area now for over a hundred years like some sort of drug lord or Mafioso. Why don't they just send a swat team into his house and—"

"They can't," Justin interrupted.

"Why not? Just blow the place up and call it a gas leak. Seems like they're pretty good at covering things up around here."

"They're afraid. Like you said, he's been terrorizing this area for more than a hundred years. There's not a family in this county who doesn't know someone who's been his victim. Sometimes it goes back generations."

"All the more reason—"

"There was a sheriff back in the '50's who went out there. Kicked in the door and gave Emerick both barrels of a 12-gauge shotgun. Saw the slugs blow holes in him you could stick your fist in. His deputies took out his friends in the house with .38 revolvers. Then they lit the house on fire and left.

"When they came back the next day, only part of the house had burned. The charred remains of Emerick's companions, familiars, feeders, whatever you want to call them, were there, but Emerick's body was nowhere to be found.

"After that, the families of two deputies started to die off. Then the deputies themselves. Then the sheriff's family. His wife, his grown kids—one of them lived with his own family in another state; they found them all dead. Not a mark on any of them. Just dead. But the sheriff knew. And he knew it was only a matter of time before Emerick came after him."

"And did he?" Lennie asked.

"They found his body in the Salem River. Folks said he drowned himself, but the man was known to be a fanatically-devout Catholic. Suicide is the last thing he would have done. It was Emerick. After that, Emerick rebuilt the damaged parts of his house and life went on just as it had before."

"He can be destroyed, Justin. I had holy water on my hands at the church and when I touched him, he cried out and his skin was scorched."

"Who's going to get close enough to douse him with it?" Justin asked. "You? With Tobias Craven by his side, he'd know you were coming a mile away."

"He's right," Max agreed. "Any thought, any plan that comes into your head is apt to be intercepted by Tobias. He's a shitty clairvoyant but he seems to have dialed into you."

"Out of desperation," Lennie told him. "Because he's in love with Emerick and he knows that's what Emerick wants." She sighed. "I've tried to block him as best I could but I can't keep it up 24/7. It's exhausting."

"Sheriff Reichert thinks it might be for the best if you just left Salem Falls."

"Left?" Max and Lennie exchanged a look.

"He wasn't the one who called you in, after all, it was the Van Helsings and they're gone. He'll think of something to tell the state police."

"What's really behind this, Justin?"

Justin studied his coffee for a long, silent moment. "Emerick has attacked his wife."

Unconsciously, Lennie touched the pardon crucifix around her neck that the sheriff's wife had given the sheriff to give her.

"Is she—"

"Dead?" Justin shook his head. "No, it's worse. She wants to go to Emerick. She's like an addict who needs their fix."

"Does the craving go away if the vampire is destroyed?"

Max asked. He knew it was a rhetorical question. No one in that room, hell, probably no one in the world, knew the definitive answer.

"I'd like to speak to Sheriff Reichert."

"Can't," Justin replied. "He's taken his wife to. . ." He hesitated. "Somewhere else," he finished, loath to say where lest Emerick find her. "Somewhere safe. . .hopefully."

"Well then, who's in charge, you?"

Justin nodded.

"I want to speak to Amalia Emerick again."

# Chapter Eleven

Lennie sat in the same cinderblock interview room she'd occupied the first time she'd spoken to the macabre relic the Portage County sheriff's department kept in their evidence room.

The mummified head of Amalia Rausch Emerick stared back at her through her dry, empty eye sockets. The parchment-like skin was falling off in flakes that littered the bottom of the wooden box in which the head was kept and the air-conditioning in the room made the strands of gray hair that had come loose from the knot at the back of the head move, giving an eerily lifelike aspect to the scene.

"Amalia," Lennie said aloud, although she didn't have to actually speak to communicate with the spirit of Balthazar's dead wife, "Will you speak to me again?"

"My husband's inamorata," came the sneering reply. "Have you come to tell me you've triumphed over me and stolen his love?"

"I'm not his inamorata, as you call it, and I don't want his love."

"Then what do you want?"

"I want to destroy him."

Amalia's cackling laughter rang in Lennie's head. "Destroy him? You have no idea how powerful he is. He cannot be destroyed."

"I think he can. I touched his face with my hand after I'd dipped it in holy water and he recoiled. It burned him. If he were to be immersed in it—"

Amalia laughed again. "Yes, that might destroy him. But you will never get him anywhere near that much holy water.

There is a church in Wellsley to the north of here that was built with a fountain in the sanctuary. A fountain of holy water. If he were to be pushed into it—"

Amalia stopped, gasping. "Balthazar. . ." the spirit wheezed.

Lennie pushed away from the table with such force that the metal chair she'd been sitting on skidded across the floor and tipped over. She backed away from the tall, powerful man dressed in black who stood in the doorway.

"Are you plotting against me Amalia?" he asked, and Lennie could see the dangerous gleam of his eyes even behind the dark lenses of his glasses. Lennie realized that the years he'd spent draining the lifeblood from Amalia gave him the ability to communicate with her spirit.

Amalia's spirit, complete with her head, materialized in the far corner of the room.

"No, Balthazar, of course not," she said, her voice trembling.

"You always were a tiresome shrew," he sneered. "You can't imagine how happy I was when you finally died."

"It's not true!" Amalia cried. "You loved me!"

"Never! I wanted your father's land, that's all. Never you. You were useless alive and now, dead, I see you've turned malicious."

"No! You loved me! I stood by while you killed my family because I knew you loved me!"

"Fool! What could I love about you? A dried-up spinster, ugly, old before her time. . ."

"No! No!"

"What could you offer me apart from your father's wealth? Nothing! You were never a mate worthy of me."

"Balthazar. . . I love you. . ." Amalia whispered, brokenly, and her spirit seemed to wither before his scorn, becoming diaphanous, wispy. She held out crabbed hands in supplication. "I love you."

"Shut up!" he shouted. Seizing the wooden box from the table, he threw it at the shadowy apparition in the corner. It hit the cinderblocks with such force that the ancient wood splintered. The head inside, dried-up and brittle, shattered into pieces that littered the tiles of the floor.

Lennie pressed herself against the wall as he turned toward her. He took off his dark glasses and his eyes glowed even in the bright light of the interrogation room. There was a red tinge to the whites, his bloodlust was rising.

"Leave me alone!" she cried. "I won't be your mate! I won't give you my power!"

"Then I'll take it," he hissed.

Crossing the space separating them too fast for the eye to follow, his hand cupped her chin and he turned her face to the side, exposing the throbbing artery in the side of her neck. Lennie struggled against him but he was too strong.

She felt his lips brush the soft skin of her throat, felt the first sharp touch of his fangs as they dug slightly into her flesh. She felt as if she were drowning, being drawn down into a bottomless pool of ecstasy like nothing she'd known in the arms of any mortal lover. This, then, was what bound his victims to him. This penetration, more intimate than the act of love, like a drug coursing in the veins. She heard him moan softly as pearls of blood swelled through the nicks he'd made in her skin. He drew back, his eyes red now, glittering.

He looked around as if seeing the world for the first time and Lennie knew he had tasted the powers of second sight inside her. His hand left her throat and caressed her cheek, like a lover.

"Stop it!" The scream came from behind them.

Startled, Balthazar turned to find the apparition of his late wife, solid now, the powers of vision he had imbibed with those few precious drops of Lennie's blood giving him the ability to see her spirit that was growing stronger, taking energy from the terror emanating from Lennie in waves. She rushed at them and began beating at Balthazar with her bloodless fists.

He stepped back to ward her off and she glanced at Lennie, watching, transfixed.

"Run!" she screamed. "Run!"

Lennie kicked the fallen chair out of her way and ran for the door. Her feet crushed the fragments of Amalia's splintered skull that covered the floor. She yanked the door open and escaped from the room, not pausing to look back at the bizarre spectacle of the struggle between the vengeful spirit and the vampire who had shattered her dreams and taken her life.

At the top of the basement stairs, she saw the crumpled corpse of Justin Leroux, his throat torn out like that of the old priest.

There was nothing she could do for him and she ran past the mournful apparition that bent over his own corpse as if unable to comprehend what had happened to him.

She shoved past the doors at the entrance to the sheriff's department and emerged into the rain. Max was waiting for her, unaware of the carnage that had just taken place inside the building. He hadn't seen Balthazar enter the building but that wasn't surprising. His vampire's powers gave him the ability to move faster than the human eye could follow when he wanted to.

"Go!" she cried, climbing into the front seat of the car beside him. "Hurry up!"

"What hap— Christ, Lennie, your neck!"

"Balthazar was there. He's killed Justin."

"He bit you?"

"He did," Lennie admitted. "But he only drank a few drops. Amalia saved me. She attacked him so I could get away."

"But Lennie..."

"Drive!" she shouted. "We have to get away from here before he overpowers Amalia! Away from Salem Falls!"

"Should be go back to the motel and get our stuff?" Max asked, starting the car.

"To hell with our stuff!"

"What about Tobias?"

"To hell with Tobias, too! Just drive, Max, drive!"

The car skidded on the wet pavement as they left the sheriff's department far behind. Max turned onto the highway and headed for the edge of town.

When they reached the dam with its earthen embankment dam, Lennie could see that the relentless rain had swelled the lake behind the dam until it overspilled its shore and was creeping toward the houses built around it. The gates were wide open, allowing a powerful rush of water to crash to the river on the other side but even that was overflowing its banks.

As they crossed, she saw the telltale cascade of water flowing out of the earthen embankment on either side of the gates.

"It's gonna go," she told Max.

"What?"

"The dam; it's going to collapse."

"Should we go back? We should warn some—"

"Too late."

Max stopped the car on the far side of the bridge that ran along the top of the dam. The cascade of water leaking out of the embankment swelled and then the embankment itself began to move, sliding down the slope toward the river.

The cascade swelled and the embankment gave way. A wall of water crashed over the ruins of the dam and before their eyes, the river became a raging torrent barreling toward Salem Falls which lay directly in its path.

"Drive, Max," Lennie said softly. "There's nothing we can do for any of them."

# Chapter Twelve

**Six Months Later**

The telephone rang as Lennie lay on the sofa in her home in Cleveland. It was Max.

"Hello, Max," she said, putting it on speaker and laying it on her chest.

"How are you doing?" he asked, from his home in Los Angeles.

"I'm all right."

"No desire to go out and suck somebody's neck?" His tone was light but she knew the question was deadly serious.

"Not really," she said, although I do get thoughts of you-know-who every once in a while."

Max was silent. He could not understand the power Balthazar Emerick had wielded over his victims. He attacked them, fed from them, and they craved him the way an addict craves their drug of choice. Even though he had extracted only a few drops of Lennie's blood, she still had moments when she longed to know what had become of him after the flood that had wiped Salem Falls off the map. When she was tempted to reach out with her mind and see if the blood he had taken from her allowed her some glimpse of his fate.

The devastation had been horrendous; the death toll had climbed into the hundreds and there was still, three months after the collapse of the dam, dozens missing.

Salem Falls was gone. Only a few foundations remained to mark the place where the houses and building had stood.

Lennie and Max had perused the pictures of the ruins until they found an image of a broken foundation labeled:

"Emerick House". The caption told of the farm's long history in Salem Falls and the house's historic significance but, the reader was assured, only a few stones of the foundation remained in place. There was even a video clip on YouTube of the ruins of the house crashing into a bridge further down the torrential river and being torn to pieces as the force of the water pushed it under the unyielding concrete and steel of the bridge structure. It emerged on the other side in fragments scarcely recognizable as having once been an ornate Victorian house.

"I'll tell you why I called," he said.

"Aw, I thought you called to see how I was," she teased.

"I did. But there's something else." He hesitated. "I'm sending you a video clip. Watch it on your computer."

"All right."

Curious, she went to her desk and switched on her computer. She opened the file Max had just sent and found herself watching a recording of one of the tabloid news shows she never watched on her own.

"Back from the dead?" a voice asked. "Tobias Craven appeared at a news conference in New York yesterday to publicize his new book, *The Vampire of Salem Falls*."

"You've got to be kidding me!" Lennie gasped.

"Keep watching," Max advised.

Tobias Craven, dapper in a black suit, his shaved head shining under the lights of the cameras trained on him, stood at a podium. To his left a table held copies of his just-released book. The cover showed a picture of a man wreathed in shadows, his red eyes gleaming out of the darkness that nearly concealed him. The drawing showed a remarkable resemblance to Balthazar Emerick.

"Mr. Craven!" a female reporter shouted. "Is it true you were held captive by a vampire?"

"It is true," Tobias assured her. "Vampires exist! I was his captive after I went to Salem Falls to investigate the stories that had persisted there for more than a century."

"Where were you when you were reported missing?" another reporter asked.

"I was being held in his home along with the rest of his victims."

"Why didn't he kill you?" a third voice asked.

"He kept me alive because he wanted to drink my blood in order to steal my powers of clairvoyance. He believed that, along with my blood, he could become a prodigious psychic."

"Oh, my God," Lennie moaned. "Listen to this. All you'd get from feeding on Tobias Craven is indigestion."

"There are rumors that the paranormal investigating team, the Van Helsing Brothers went to Salem Falls to try and help you."

"I believe they were there," Tobias allowed, "although I had no contact with them. To my knowledge, however, they haven't spoken publicly about the matter."

"I've heard one of them is under a psychiatrist's care at a private hospital in an undisclosed location."

"Again", Tobias said with a dismissive wave of one pale, elegant hand, "I've heard nothing about them. They would be of little interest to the vampire since it was psychic ability he was looking for."

"Can you believe the *cajones* on this guy?" Max marveled, listening to the soundtrack on Lennie's computer over the phone.

"He never gives up." Lennie agreed.

"Has the vampire been destroyed?" the female reporter who'd asked the first question said, raising her hand.

"He has been defeated," Tobias assured her with a smug smile. "I can't reveal more; who would want to read my book?"

"Who wants to read it anyway?" Max grumbled.

"I do," Lennie said with a laugh. "And he'd better hope you-know-who is gone. He'll go after Tobias with a vengeance after this."

"I wouldn't mind that," Max admitted. "But I don't want him going after you. Tell me he's gone for good, Lennie. Tell me he was swept away in the flood and destroyed."

"I can't tell you that, Max, because I don't know. I just hope if he is still around, he stays far away from me."

"Promise me you'll keep some holy water handy."

"I'll get a gallon," Lennie assured him.

"Promise me something else, Lennie."

"What's that?"

"If we ever get into a position like we did in Louisiana where Tobias is depending on us to save his life, we'll just walk away."

"I promise," Lennie laughed, and switched off the computer shutting Tobias up in mid-boast.

**The End**

# About the Author

**Larry Scholl** grew up in Chicago, Illinois and lived for many years on Beaver Island, the most remote inhabited island in Lake Michigan. He now lives in southern central Michigan where he enjoys writing and collecting and selling antiques, particularly vintage toy trucks.

He is the author of eight previous books, ***The House Where I Died, Undead: The Vampire of Killbryde Castle,*** novels featuring Max Lovecraft and Lennie McMann including ***Devil's Night—The Haunting of Fitz Mansion, Don't Fear the Reaper, Suffer, the Little Children, The Keeper,*** and ***Zombies Awaken*** and one work of non-fiction, ***True Stories of Haunted People, Places, and Things Volume One,*** all of which are available for Kindle and in other formats on Amazon.com.

He welcomes questions or comments at:

larryscholl@aol.com

Made in the USA
Columbia, SC
07 February 2025